ODYSSEUS AND THE CYCLOPS

CIRCE ENCHANTS ODYSSEUS

THE CALL OF THE SIRENS

THREE TALES FROM *THE ODYSSEY*

retold by Jeannette Sanderson

Table of Contents

MYTHS

What is a myth?

A myth (MITH) is a story that explains something that occurs in nature. It might tell how the world began or explain why the world is the way it is. The main character in a myth is usually a god or goddess or a hero with special powers. Sometimes the hero in a myth is on a quest (KWEST), a journey in search of adventure.

What is the purpose of a myth?

Long ago, people believed myths to be true. They relied on these stories to explain events they did not understand, like violent storms or why there is night and day. Today myths help us see what events confused or interested people long ago. The explanations in myths are creative and fun. They are exciting, too.

How do you read a myth?

The title of a myth often tells what event in nature the myth explains. Think about how the event is explained when you read a myth. Look for a hero with extraordinary powers. Ask yourself, *What does this hero do? How do the hero's actions help explain an event?*

Who invented myths?

In ancient times, storytellers told myths to answer questions about the world. Their listeners understood the heroes of these

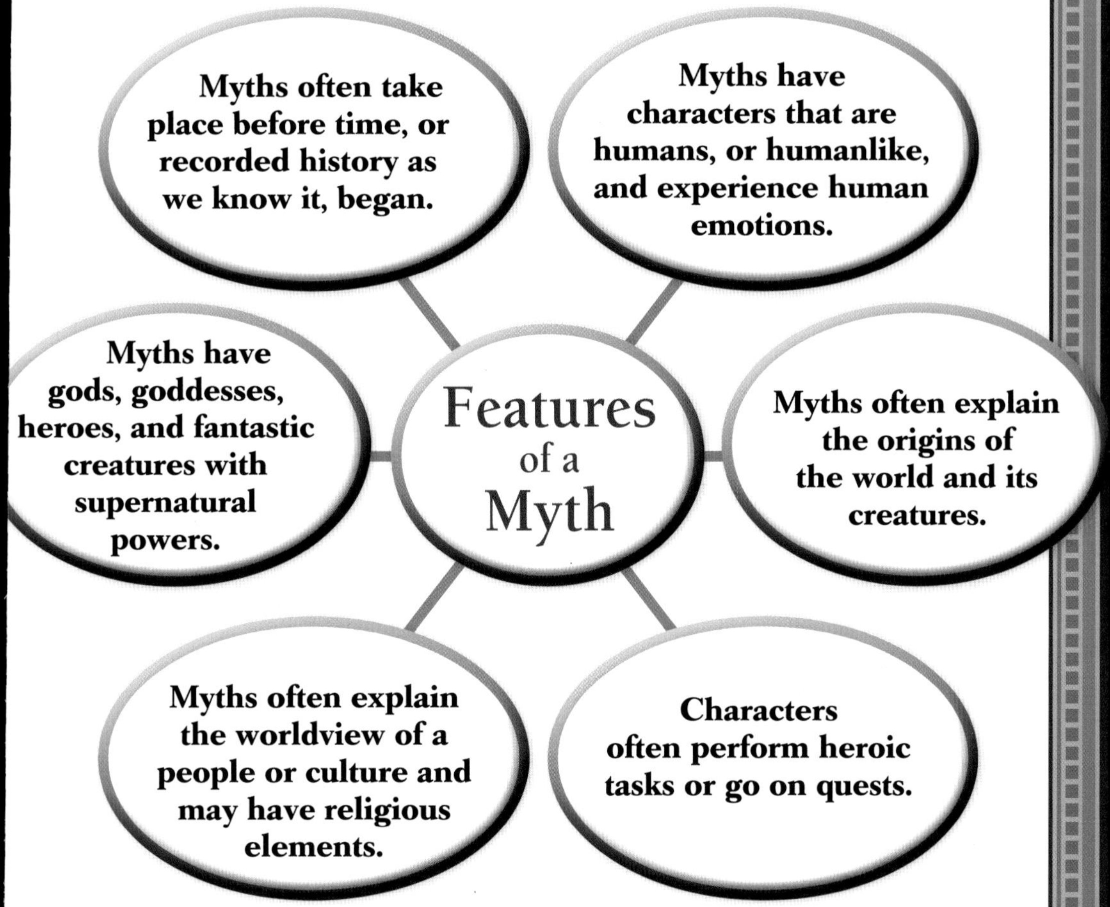

Features of a Myth

- Myths often take place before time, or recorded history as we know it, began.
- Myths have characters that are humans, or humanlike, and experience human emotions.
- Myths have gods, goddesses, heroes, and fantastic creatures with supernatural powers.
- Myths often explain the origins of the world and its creatures.
- Myths often explain the worldview of a people or culture and may have religious elements.
- Characters often perform heroic tasks or go on quests.

myths. They were heroes with human qualities similar to their own, but their superpowers meant that they could perform amazing deeds. In an ancient Greek myth, the god Prometheus gives humans the gift of fire. Another myth about the Greek goddess Demeter explains the change of seasons. The Mexican god Quetzalcoatl takes a dangerous journey to his homeland in a myth. As the centuries passed, these stories were told and retold and then written down. Today science has explained the events in myths, but readers still enjoy the exciting adventures of these heroes.

TOOLS FOR READERS AND WRITERS

Metaphor

A metaphor compares two things that are seemingly unalike. Metaphors directly describe something often using the word **is** or **was** rather than **like** or **as**. Authors use metaphors to help readers create vivid images that helps them see, or be, where the story takes place. Authors of myths often use metaphors to show how characters or objects resemble or represent something else.

Heterographs

Heterographs are words that are pronounced the same or sound alike, but are spelled differently and have different meanings. Examples are **pear**, **pair**, and **pare** and **write**, **rite**, and **wright**. These soundalike words can be confusing; readers need to read carefully to know which heterograph the author is using.

Summarize Information

A summary is a brief retelling of the story's plot without any dialogue. To help readers remember what they have read, they should summarize as they read. Good readers often write down important events and details as they read, keeping these notes short and to the point. Sometimes an important event is identified in one paragraph and developed through following paragraphs.

Athena

BACKGROUND ON *THE ODYSSEY*

Odysseus* was a legendary hero who helped the Greeks win the Trojan War around 1200 B.C.E. After ten years of fighting, Odysseus was relieved to finally set sail from the ancient city of Troy to his island home of Ithaca, off the west coast of Greece. He was looking forward to seeing his wife and son. He expected a quick and uneventful journey home.

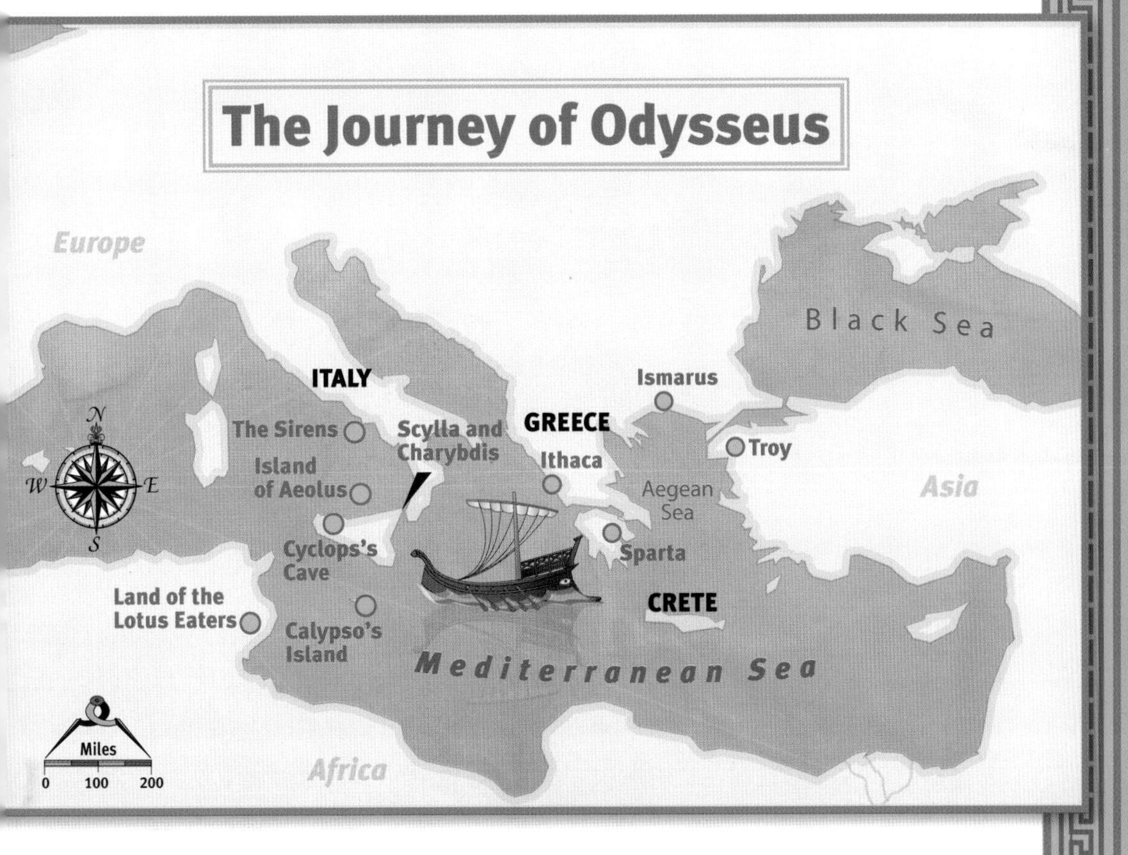

***In Roman mythology, Odysseus is known as Ulysses.**

The gods, who often meddled in humans' affairs, had other plans. The goddess Athena had helped Odysseus and the Greeks win the Trojan War. Instead of worshipping at the goddess's altar, however, some of the Greek warriors were violent in her temple in Troy. The gods were so angry at this disrespect that they wanted to destroy the Greek ships.

Zeus

Zeus, the king of the gods, threw thunderbolts at the ships. Poseidon, god of the sea, sent giant waves crashing over them and Odysseus's men were tossed about the violent seas. Further angered by Odysseus's bragging, Poseidon delayed Odysseus's journey home for another ten years with a host of deadly obstacles.

Poseidon

The Odyssey is a collection of twenty-four stories recounting Odysseus's adventures after the fall of Troy and his attempt to go home. He battles giants, witches, and other strange creatures, and he is often forced to perform arduous tasks that require both strength and cunning to complete. In English, as well as many other languages, *odyssey* means "an epic (very long) trip."

As with other Greek myths, the original stories about Odysseus began as an oral poetic tradition. They were first written down by the poet Homer around the eighth century B.C.E.

Homer

ODYSSEUS AND THE CYCLOPS

Odysseus had left Troy years ago with a dozen ships and many men. But rough seas threw his ships off course, and Odysseus and his fleet had to stop at islands along the way to replenish their supply of food and fresh water. They had only recently escaped from the sleepy land of the Lotus-eaters. Now, unbeknownst to them, they docked on the island of the Cyclops, a dreaded, one-eyed giant.

Odysseus

Odysseus, a brave man, chose from his crew twelve other men of **mettle** and set off to explore the island. They brought with them a jar of wine that Apollo's priest had given them; they would give it as a gift to whoever lived on the island.

After walking for some time, Odysseus and his men came to a giant cave surrounded by sheep. "Where is the shepherd?" asked Eurylochus, Odysseus's lieutenant.

"Let us go inside the cave," said Odysseus. "Perhaps we will find him there."

There was no shepherd inside the cave, but there were wheels of cheese as tall as the tallest soldier and buckets of milk big enough for all of the men to bathe in.

"This shepherd must be a giant!" said a crewman named Elpenor.

Suddenly, a shadow fell across the mouth of the cave. Odysseus and his men turned and saw a horrific sight: an ugly, one-eyed giant stood at the entrance to the cave, blocking their exit.

"Who trespasses in my home?" roared the giant. "Did you not see the **gate**?"

"We are Greek warriors," said Odysseus. "We have stopped here on our long journey home from Troy—"

"Silence! Do you not know that I am Polyphemus, son of Poseidon, god of the sea? Do you not know that this is my home?"

"If this is your home," said Odysseus, "then we are your guests. Where is your hospitality?"

The giant's laugh was thunder. "Hospitality? Do you expect me to have you to dinner? Ha! I will have you *for* dinner, and for breakfast and lunch as well." And with that, Polyphemus grabbed two of Odysseus's men and gobbled them up. "There is my hospitality," he said with a belch. Then the Cyclops brought his sheep inside his cave for the night and blocked the entrance with a giant boulder.

the Cyclops

Odysseus's men trembled with fear. "We are trapped," they whispered to their leader. "The Cyclops will eat us! What shall we do?" But Odysseus was as clever as he was brave. He quickly thought of a way to prevent Polyphemus from eating any more of his men.

"Polyphemus, you must be thirsty after your dinner. Please drink this wine I brought for you."

"Wine? Give me that!" said Polyphemus. He took a giant gulp. "This is liquid joy," he said. "I must find a way to thank you for it. Tell me your name."

Odysseus had his answer ready. "My name," he said, "is Nobody."

Polyphemus gave a drowsy nod. "To thank you for your wine, Nobody, I will eat the rest of your men first. I will eat Nobody last. Now leave me be. The wine has made me sleepy."

As soon as Polyphemus fell asleep, Odysseus directed his

men to a giant olive tree branch near the rear of the cave. "Take out your knives," he said. "We must work quickly, before the Cyclops awakens."

The men worked until they had sharpened one end of the branch to a fine point. Then Odysseus and his men hefted the branch and ran toward the sleeping Polyphemus. They drove the spear right into the Cyclops's eye, blinding him.

"Oh, my eye, my eye!" Polyphemus roared. "Brother, help me!"

Moments later, the ground outside the cave shook fiercely. The approaching Cyclops's footsteps were small earthquakes.

"His brother is coming. Now we are surely doomed," said another sailor.

"Hush," said Odysseus. "You will see. We will be safe in the cave."

A loud voice bellowed from outside the cave. "Why have you woken me, Polyphemus? Who is harming you?"

"Nobody is harming me!" shouted Polyphemus.

"Then why did you wake me?"

"Nobody is killing me!" Polyphemus shouted.

"Then why are you screaming so?"

"Nobody has blinded me!" Polyphemus cried.

Brother Cyclops kicked the boulder so hard that stones fell from the roof of the cave. "You speak foolishly, Polyphemus. If nobody is harming you, then I am going back to sleep." And Brother Cyclops stormed off.

Polyphemus cried out in agony. "I will get you for this, Nobody. You will never get past me alive!"

"Your wisdom saved us from Brother Cyclops," whispered Elpenor. "But how are we going to get out of the cave?"

"Do not worry," said Odysseus. "I will think of something."

Soon it was morning. Polyphemus moved the boulder to let his sheep go out and graze. The blinded giant stood in the entryway and carefully felt the backs of his woolly sheep as they passed through the cave's opening.

"Beware, Nobody! My sheep are the only beings that will leave this cave alive!"

Odysseus noticed that Polyphemus felt only the backs of his sheep; he never checked their bellies. He quickly directed his men to twist their hands and feet into the sheep's thick belly fleece, and ride underneath the animals to get out of the cave. His plan worked! Soon, Odysseus and his men were outside the cave.

The men dropped from the sheep's bellies and headed back to the ship at a quick **gait**, driving the Cyclops's flock before them. The waiting crew was saddened to learn what the Cyclops had done to several of their comrades.

"I am sorry most of all," said Odysseus, "for they were my men. But we cannot change what has happened; we must look to the future. Let us board our ship quickly, before the Cyclops notices we are gone."

When they were a safe distance from shore, Odysseus stood up in the boat. "Polyphemus!" he called. "Polyphemus! We have escaped, and we have taken your sheep!"

The Cyclops thundered to the shore, picked up a giant boulder, and threw it toward the sound of Odysseus's voice. "Take that, Nobody!" he shouted.

"I am not Nobody!" Odysseus shouted.

Polyphemus picked up another boulder, and Odysseus's men begged him to leave the angry giant alone. But Odysseus's pride made him speak. "It was not nobody who blinded you; it was Odysseus, king of Ithaca."

Polyphemus dropped to his knees. "Father Poseidon, hear me. Odysseus blinded me. Punish him! Make his journey as miserable as I am now!" Then Polyphemus stood and hurled one last boulder at Odysseus's ship. The boulder sent a giant wave that pushed Odysseus and his men farther out to sea.

The waters became peaceful, and Odysseus looked around him. Had Poseidon heard his son's call? Odysseus knew that the gods liked to **meddle** in human affairs. Would Poseidon punish Odysseus for blinding Polyphemus? Or would Odysseus have smooth sailing for the rest of his journey home? Odysseus prayed to the gods it would be the latter.

REREAD THE MYTH

Analyze the Characters and Plot

- Who are the main characters in the myth?
- Who are the minor characters in the myth?
- Who is Polyphemus? How does his lineage play into the myth?
- On page 13, the crew begs Odysseus to leave the giant alone. Odysseus does not. What do his actions tell you about Odysseus?
- How does the myth end?

Focus on Comprehension: Summarize Information

- Which important events should be included in a summary of the first day of the myth?
- Odysseus tricked Polyphemus twice. Summarize each event and explain its consequences.
- In one sentence, summarize the last paragraph of the myth.

Focus on Antagonists

Greek myths often include an antagonist: a main character who opposes a myth's hero or protagonist.

- Who is the antagonist in this myth?
- How does the antagonist oppose Odysseus?
- What negative character traits does the antagonist possess?

Analyze the Tools Writers Use: Metaphor

- On page 9, the author says that the giant's laugh is thunder. What does the author mean?
- On page 10, the author says the wine is liquid joy. Describe what "liquid joy" might mean.
- On page 11, the author says that Brother Cyclops's footsteps are small earthquakes approaching the cave. Why does the author say the footsteps are "small earthquakes"? Why not "large earthquakes"?

Focus on Words: Heterographs

Make a chart like the one below. For each word, identify its part of speech. Then identify the heterograph's definition. Finally, identify words from the text that helped you determine which heterograph the author used.

Page	Word	Part of Speech	Definition	Text Words That Helped Determine Meaning
8	mettle			
13	meddle			
9	gate			
12	gait			

CIRCE ENCHANTS ODYSSEUS

Poseidon heard Polyphemus's cries. Poseidon heard his Cyclops son ask him to make Odysseus's journey miserable as vengeance for blinding him. Since Poseidon held **reign** over the seas, the god punished Odysseus with rough sailing. By the time Odysseus had reached Circe's island, eleven of his twelve ships had been destroyed.

"We will find food and fresh water to continue our journey home," Odysseus told his charges as they came ashore. "But we must be careful. We have lost too many of our men already."

When he spotted a castle in the distance, Odysseus called to Eurylochus. "Take half of our men and see who lives in that castle. Then report back to me."

The scouting party walked until they got near enough to the castle to see that wolves and lions surrounded it. The men were wondering what to do when a beautiful woman stepped out of the castle.

"**Rein** in your wild animals!" one of the men called out.

"Do not be afraid, travelers," she said. "I am Circe and these men—I mean, these animals—are my pets. They are completely harmless."

When the sailors saw the wolves wag their tails, they began to relax. Eurylochus kept his guard up, however. He slipped behind a tree and quietly cautioned his men to be careful.

"Are you afraid of a lion that purrs?" one of the men teasingly asked.

"It's that woman. I don't trust her. Those animals seem almost . . . human."

"Come with me," Circe said with a reassuring smile. "Be my guests. You look hungry and tired. I will feed you, and then you can rest."

Eurylochus tried to keep his men from going to the beautiful woman, but they ignored his whispered pleas. So he kept himself hidden behind the tree and watched as his men wolfed down the mounds of food Circe put in front of them.

Circe

"This food is delicious!" said one of the men with his mouth full. "I hope you have more!"

"Yes, lots more!" added another of the men as he grabbed another chunk of cheese.

Circe's face became a thundercloud. She shook her head in disgust and pulled a long stick from her sleeve. "You are pigs," she said, "and pigs you shall become." She tapped each man with her wand, and the men turned to swine.

Eurylochus watched in disbelief as his men were turned into pigs. Then he hurried back to Odysseus.

"There is a **vile** enchantress who lives on this island!" The words tumbled out of Eurylochus's mouth. "She has turned our men into pigs!"

"What?!" Odysseus cried in disbelief. Then he was an angry bull. "I will find that enchantress and make her turn my charges back into men!" He hurried off toward the castle. On his way, Hermes, messenger of the gods, appeared before him.

"The goddess Athena has sent me to help you. She bids you take this herb so that Circe's magic will not affect you." Hermes handed Odysseus a **vial**, and he drank from it.

"Thank you," the grateful Odysseus said. "And please thank the goddess Athena upon your return to Olympus."

When Odysseus reached the castle, he found it surrounded by lions, wolves, and pigs. Just as before, the beautiful Circe came out to greet her guest, smiling her deceptive smile.

"Welcome to my castle," she said. "I am Circe. Sit and rest. I will feed you."

"Thank you, Circe. You are most kind." Odysseus returned his own deceptive smile. Then he proceeded to eat the bread and cheese that Circe gave him. He drank her wine. When he finished, Circe tapped him with her magic wand. Nothing happened. She tapped him again. Still nothing.

"What is happening? Why aren't you turning into a boar?"

Odysseus leaped to his feet. "You cannot harm me, you vile enchantress, but my sword can harm you!" Odysseus pulled out his sword and held it to Circe's neck. "You turned my men into pigs! I demand that you turn them back into men!"

"Put your sword away. I am sure you do not wish to harm me."

"I do not wish to harm any woman," said the gallant Odysseus, "but it is my duty to protect my men. Please release them from your spell."

Sighing, Circe tapped each of the pigs with her wand. As she did so, they turned back into men.

"Thank you," said Odysseus. "Now we must continue on our journey home."

"Wait," said Circe. "Because you have shown yourself to be a noble leader, I wish to warn you of the dangers that await you. Beware the Sirens, beautiful creatures that are part bird and part human. Their enchanted songs lure sailors to their island. Their ships crash on the rocks and the sailors die. You must also beware the monsters Charybdis and Scylla. One lives in the bottom of a whirlpool, the other in a cave. Both will try to destroy you."

"Thank you for the warnings," said Odysseus. "Your advice will be our compass. Now we must be on our way."

REREAD THE MYTH

Analyze the Characters and Plot

- Who are the main characters in the myth?
- Who are the minor characters in the myth?
- Circe is probably a witch. How can you tell?
- Eurylochus's men ate like pigs, so Circe turned them into pigs. What do you think the men did who were turned into lions and wolves?
- Why is Hermes such an important part of this myth?
- What does Circe do at the end of the myth that shows consideration for others?

Focus on Comprehension: Summarize Information

- The author says the scouting party comes to a castle and meets Circe. Summarize what happens next in two to three sentences.
- In three to four sentences, summarize what happens when Odysseus goes to the castle.
- In two sentences, summarize the myth's ending.

Focus on Antagonists

Remember that Greek myths usually include antagonists who oppose the myth's hero, or protagonist.

- Who is the antagonist in this myth?
- How does the antagonist oppose Odysseus?
- What negative character traits does the antagonist possess?
- What positive character traits does the antagonist possess?

Analyze the Tools Writers Use: Metaphor

- On page 17, the author says that Circe's face becomes a thundercloud. What might her face have looked like?
- On page 18, the author says Odysseus is an angry bull. Would you want to be around Odysseus in this state? Why or why not?
- On page 19, Odysseus tells Circe that her advice will be their compass. What does Odysseus mean by this?

Focus on Words: Heterographs

Make a chart like the one below. For each word, identify its part of speech. Then identify the heterograph's definition. Finally, identify words from the text that helped you determine which heterograph the author used.

Page	Word	Part of Speech	Definition	Text Words That Helped Determine Meaning
16	reign			
16	rein			
18	vile			
18	vial			

The Call of the Sirens

The author introduces an obstacle/task that Odysseus, the hero, must overcome. Fantastical creatures, such as Sirens, are often found in myths.

The enchantress Circe had warned Odysseus about the Sirens. These part-bird, part-human creatures with a **flair** for magical, mystical song caused sailors to crash their ships on the rocky shores of their island. Odysseus resolved to protect the men on his one remaining ship from this fate, even if it cost him his life.

"We are approaching the island of the Sirens," Odysseus told his men. "I must keep you from hearing their magical songs. Otherwise, you will be lured to a certain death."

"We are stronger than that. We will not be taken in by the Sirens' tricks," his men argued.

"No," said Odysseus, "as your leader, I cannot allow you to hear them. You will protect yourselves by filling your ears with beeswax."

"But what about you?" asked Eurylochus.

Because this is a myth, the author shows Odysseus's heroic qualities: He'll risk his life for his men.

"You will tie me to the mast. I will be the first man to hear the Sirens' song and live to tell about it. You will release me when we are well past the island, but not before then, no matter what I do or say."

The men filled their ears with beeswax. They secured their leader to the ship's mast.

The plot is in motion. The Sirens are singing. What will happen? How will the hero respond?

Just as the last knot was tightened, the Sirens' voices began to fill the air.

"Odysseus, bravest of Greek heroes, come hear our song," sang a luscious chorus of angelic voices.

Odysseus became hypnotized. His eyes flew open wide; he threw his head from side to side. He was desperate to hear more of the Sirens' song. His frantic desire caused his nostrils to **flare** and his breath to quicken.

"Bring your ship to our island," they sang. "We will fill your ears with heavenly music."

Odysseus tugged at the ropes that bound him, but they wouldn't loosen. "Oh, how can creatures with such lovely voices do us harm? Release me! Release me! The Sirens are calling my name."

Odysseus's men were deaf to his **pleas**. They went about the business of sailing. As they passed the island of the Sirens, they shook their heads at all the skeletons scattered about on the island, and they prayed to the gods for a wind that would quickly carry them away from such a terrible place.

the Sirens

Meanwhile, the Sirens kept up their calls. "Come to us and give yourselves rest. Our sweet voices will soothe you; our songs will bring you peace."

Here, the author shows Odysseus's pain in his dialogue rather than telling the reader that he is in pain.

Odysseus called on all the gods of Mount Olympus to help him. "**Please**, gods, help me! Can't you see the pain I am in? Release me from my binds so that I may go to these worthy creatures."

But the gods were as deaf to his pleas as his own men. Still, the Sirens taunted him.

"Oh, powerful Odysseus, most famed of Greek heroes, surely you can break those ropes," they sang.

Here the author describes the hero's actions (his pain) so that the reader can create his or her own mental image.

Odysseus shouted for the gods, for his men, for anyone to free him. He struggled so mightily against the ropes that his wrists and ankles bled. But his men had served him well; there was no breaking free of his binds.

When the island was no longer visible, Eurylochus untied his leader from the mast. Odysseus fell to the deck, exhausted.

"Did you see all the skeletons on the island's rocky shore?" Eurylochus asked.

"No," Odysseus answered. "I only heard the Sirens' bewitching song. It was beautiful, yet terrible."

"You saved us yet again," one of his men said. "But look ahead. The waters on the left appear very rough. Shall we stay near the cave on the right?"

The author develops the plot. The hero escapes one challenge but must immediately face another. The author has constructed this story with one adventure after another because it is an epic—a series of adventures that covers a long period of time.

Odysseus's mind had become a fog during the Sirens' songs. He shook his head to clear it and remembered Circe's other warnings. He knew that the rough seas must be the whirlpool monster, Charybdis. He also knew that the cave must be the home of the six-headed Scylla. Had he come this far only to choose which way his men would die?

The whirlpool began to tug at the ship. "To the right, men, steer to the right!" Odysseus called out. With great effort, the men pulled themselves out of the whirlpool's grasp. They were congratulating themselves when a monster with six ugly heads peered out of the cave.

Myths often have action scenes.

"Faster, men! Row faster!" Odysseus called as he lifted three spears in each hand. As the monster opened each of its mouths and leaned toward his ship, Odysseus threw all six spears at it. The spears were mere toothpicks to the monster, and the men were but toothsome appetizers. Scylla grabbed a man with each of its heads and proceeded to crush each one between its sharp teeth.

Fearful of losing even more men, Odysseus picked up an oar and began rowing himself. "Keep rowing! Harder! Harder!" he shouted.

The author shows that Odysseus is not just an action hero. He is a complicated character who has to make a difficult decision, and it weighs on him heavily.

Soon they were beyond the whirlpool and the cave.

"We made it!" Eurylochus said.

"Not soon enough," Odysseus said. The brave leader was crying. "Those were my men. They trusted their lives to me."

"You are too hard on yourself, Odysseus. If we

the monsters Charybdis and Scylla

had steered away from the monster, we would all have perished in the whirlpool. You saved as many men as you could."

Odysseus looked up to the sky and shook his head. "Let us continue our journey," he said. "Let us see what else the gods have in store for us. On to Ithaca, men!"

Ithaca was an island of ancient Greece. This last sentence (as well as the type of simple boat Odysseus's men row) reminds the reader that the myth takes place long ago.

Analyze the Characters and Plot

- Who are the main characters in the myth?
- Who are the minor characters in the myth?
- Odysseus does not let his men even try to be strong against the Sirens' powers. What might these actions say about Odysseus?
- What role do the ropes play in Odysseus's survival?
- Why does Odysseus not see the skeletons on the island?
- Odysseus saves all but six men. What happens to these six men?

▲ Odysseus's ship near the island of the Sirens

Focus on Comprehension: Summarize Information

- In two to three sentences, summarize the first part of the myth until the men fill their ears with beeswax.
- What important events should be included in a summary about Odysseus surviving the Sirens?
- Write a three-to-four sentence paragraph summarizing the ending of the myth when Odysseus and his men survive the whirlpool and the six-headed Scylla.

Focus on Antagonists

Remember that Greek myths usually include antagonists who oppose the myth's hero, or protagonist.

- Who are the antagonists in this myth?
- How do the antagonists oppose Odysseus?
- What negative character traits does the antagonist possess?

Analyze the Tools Writers Use: Metaphor

- On page 25, the author says that Odysseus's mind has become a fog. Why did the author choose these words to describe Odysseus's mind?
- On page 25, the author says the spears Odysseus throws at the monster are mere toothpicks to the monster and that Odysseus's men are but toothsome appetizers for the monster. What do these words and phrases say about the monster's size?

Focus on Words: Heterographs

Make a chart like the one below. For each word, identify its part of speech. Then identify the heterograph's definition. Finally, identify words from the text that helped you determine which heterograph the author used.

Page	Word	Part of Speech	Definition	Text Words That Helped Determine Meaning
22	flair			
23	flare			
23	pleas			
24	please			

How does an author write a MYTH?

Reread "The Call of the Sirens" and think about what Jeannette Sanderson did to retell this myth. How did she develop the story? How can you, as a writer, develop your own retelling of a myth?

1. Research Myths and Decide on One to Retell

Many cultures have their own myths and gods. First, decide on the culture whose myths you want to research. You may want to focus on one particular god or hero you already know about. Writers learn as much as they can about the myth they want to retell and often read different versions in books or from online sources. While you read the different versions of the myth, think about parts you will retell and which parts you will leave out.

2. Identify and Develop Characters

Writers ask these questions:

- Who are the major and minor characters in this myth?
- What type of god or hero is the main character? What special skills does he or she have?
- What human traits does each character possess?
- What words can I choose to develop the characters' traits?
- How will character traits affect the plot?

Characters	Type of God/ Hero	Traits	Examples
Odysseus	leader of a ship	intelligent, responsible, brave	ensures the safety of his men but puts himself in danger while passing by the Sirens
Sirens	half-bird, half-woman daughters of a water god	beautiful with magical voices, but evil	lure sailors with enchanting song so the ships crash on their rocky island
Scylla	six-headed sea monster	ravenous, dangerous	eats as many of Odysseus's men as it can when the ship passes by

3. Rethink Setting and Plot

Myths, like other fiction stories, have a setting and a plot. When you write a retelling of a myth, you have to be familiar with where and when the original story takes place, the problem and events of the story, and the solution to the problem. Then you can choose your own words in the retelling.

Setting	the Mediterranean Sea, thousands of years ago
Problem of the Story	Odysseus needs to pilot his ship past deadly creatures.
Story Events	1. Circe warns Odysseus about the Sirens, whose song lures sailors to crash their ships. 2. Odysseus orders his men to stuff their ears with beeswax and tie him tightly to the mast with his ears free to hear the Sirens' song. 3. Odysseus hears the enchanting song and tries to change his orders, but he cannot because he is tied tightly and his men can't hear him. 4. The ship passes the Sirens safely. 5. Odysseus must choose one evil over another: He avoids the whirlpool of Charybdis by steering toward the man-eating monster Scylla.
Solution to the Problem	Odysseus and his men pull together to row past the monster as quickly as possible but still end up losing a few men. From there, they continue on their journey home.

GLOSSARY

flair (FLAIR) special ability (page 22)

flare (FLAIR) to widen (page 23)

gait (GATE) pace of walking (page 12)

gate (GATE) barrier that opens and closes (page 9)

meddle (MEH-dul) be interested in someone else's concern (page 13)

mettle (MEH-tul) strength of spirit (page 8)

pleas (PLEEZ) earnest requests (page 23)

please (PLEEZ) word that expresses a polite request (page 24)

reign (RANE) royal authority (page 16)

rein (RANE) to hold back (page 16)

vial (VILE) small tube (page 18)

vile (VILE) evil (page 18)